City at Night

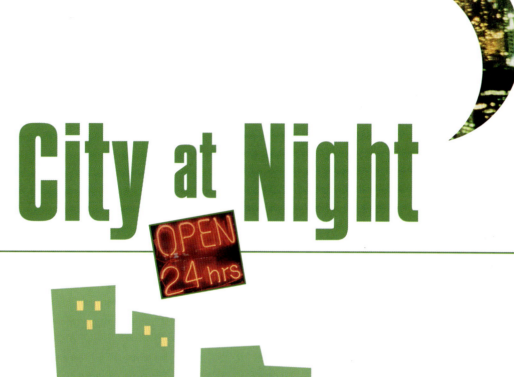

Peter Jestadt

with text by Karen Millyard

Annick Press • Toronto • New York

©1998 Peter Jestadt (concept and photography)
©1998 Karen Millyard (text)
©1998 Gary Lawrence (additional photography, Vancouver)
Co-ordinator/researcher: Anna-Louise Richardson
Design: Sheryl Shapiro
Consultant: Judy Diehl
Endpaper photography: Hot Shots Stock Shots, Toronto, and Peter Jestadt

Annick Press Ltd.
All rights reserved. No part of this work covered by the copyrights hereon may be reproduced or used in any form or by any means – graphic, electronic, or mechanical – without the prior written permission of the publisher.

 We acknowledge the support of the Canada Council for the Arts for our publishing program. We also thank the Ontario Arts Council.

Cataloguing in Publication Data
Jestadt, Peter,
    City at night

ISBN 1-55037-549-0

1. Night work – Juvenile literature. 2. Occupations – Juvenile literature.
I. Millyard, Karen. II. Title.

HD5113.J47 1998   j331.25'74   C98-930833-2

The text in this book was typeset in Apollo.

Distributed in Canada by:	Published in the U.S.A. by Annick Press (U.S.) Ltd.
Firefly Books Ltd.	Distributed in the U.S.A. by:
3680 Victoria Park Avenue	Firefly Books (U.S.) Inc.
Willowdale, ON	P.O. Box 1338
M2H 3K1	Ellicott Station
	Buffalo, NY 14205

Printed and bound in Canada by Metropole, Montréal, Québec

Introduction

Great cities resemble one another at night. After the sun goes down, sights, sounds and smells are much alike in New York, Toronto, Chicago, Montreal and Vancouver. On a hot summer night, the sound of window air-conditioners might mix with voices and music coming from a club or coffee shop, sirens in the distance, and a plane flying low overhead. There are rippling reflections of harbour lights in the water, familiar shadows, the smell of damp pavement.

By now, the end of the twentieth century, most of North America's population has become urban. Cities are the places where most of us live and work, day *or* night.

This book celebrates the life of the city after dark and the contribution of the night worker. Besides hospital staff, firefighters and the police force, just who *are* the people keeping the city a clean and safe place, contributing to other people's health, joy and comfort?

One day Peter Jestadt took his camera and set out to visit four cities at night, and he photographed their faces.

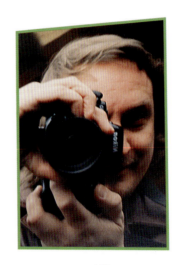

For Alice.
—Peter Jestadt

"I'll take a picture of anything that interests me, like my warped reflection in a car window."

Contents

8:00 p.m.	The Aquabus	6
8:30 p.m.	The Masters' Swim Club	8
9:00 p.m.	The Book Fair	10
9:30 p.m.	Island Airport	12
10:00 p.m.	The Theatre	14
10:30 p.m.	The Concert	16
11:00 p.m.	Union Station	18
11:30 p.m.	Sarah's Café	20
12:00 a.m.	Hotel Bonaventure	22
12:30 a.m.	The Hospital	24
1:00 a.m.	Times Square	26
1:30 a.m.	A Newspaper	28
2:00 a.m.	The Street Patrol	30
2:30 a.m.	The Subway	32
3:00 a.m.	24-Hour Grocery Store	34
3:30 a.m.	The All-Night Bus	36
4:00 a.m.	Amy's Bread	38
4:30 a.m.	A Farmers' Market	40
5:00 a.m.	*Metro Morning* Radio	42
5:30 a.m.	A Construction Site	44
6:00 a.m.	The Wildlife Centre	46

The Aquabus
8:00 p.m.

The Aquabus carries people across False Creek, a salt-water inlet in downtown Vancouver.

Captain Vasquez piloting the Aquabus.

A breeze is blowing across the water and making little patterns on the dark, flashing surface. A group of people stand on the dock, waiting for the ferry to arrive.

Vancouver, sitting right on the Pacific Ocean, is a city of water. Many people in the communities along that part of the coast have only one way of reaching each other: by water. The boats play an important role in their lives every single day.

The pilots have to concentrate as they steer their way through the crowded waters—there are kayaks, sailboats and rowboats to watch out for.

In the summer, many of the passengers are tourists. The pilots answer questions about the city, the sights, good places to eat, and the wildlife, including eagles, seals, and many kinds of water birds.

The boat bumps lightly against the dock. "Hi, John," says one of the regular passengers, settling down to enjoy the last spectacular ride of the evening. A loon calls in the dark. It's a beautiful night.

The Masters' Swim Club
8:30 p.m.

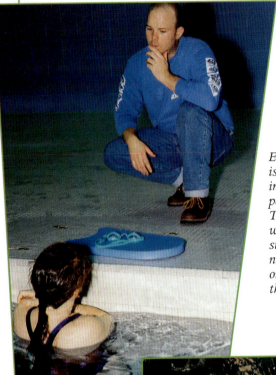

Each workout is designed to improve a particular skill. The coaches write the strokes and the number of laps on a board by the pool.

The youngest members are 20, the oldest over 100, with swimmers competing against people within a five-year age range.

Inside the large concrete building there is a room with humid, chlorine-scented air. A whistle shrieks and the swimmers lunge forward, their arms chopping the water into dancing waves.

The swim club meets several times a week. Masters' swimmers are adult competitive swimmers. They are a mixed group: some are ex-Olympic athletes and some are purely recreational. They belong to clubs all over the world. What they all have in common, though, is their dedication and hard work.

The coaches, some of them volunteer, are there to run the practice. They do their job in the evening so that the swimmers, who go to work or school or look after their families during the day, can fit the regular workouts into their schedules. The coaches help the swimmers by giving them advice on their starts, strokes, turns and pacing, and preparing them for swim meets.

The whistle blows again, and the swimmers relax. The workout is over, and they begin their "cool-down", looking forward to a hot shower.

The Book Fair
9:00 p.m.

Writers and illustrators come to autograph copies of their new books.

They also give readings and sometimes hold question-and-answer sessions.

The sun has gone down, and the Salon du Livre in Montreal has just begun. Inside the great building, the lights are bright and hot, the booths are full of colourful books, and hundreds of people are ready to do business. Downstairs, long lines of people stand waiting to buy tickets.

The Salon is a book fair. French-language publishers and book-sellers come here from all over the world to meet, talk about books, buy and sell. They will be working at the fair till very late this evening, and for the next five days they will work from ten in the morning until ten at night.

But this is also a people's fair—a celebration of books and reading! On Children's Day, the aisles fill with school kids excited about all the new children's books that are shown here for the very first time. Families come too, with toddlers and grandparents and everyone in between. If it weren't for the Salon, some people might never have a chance to meet an author or illustrator.

More people are arriving. The doors swing wide, just like the cover of a book ... and let them into the wonderful world inside.

Island Airport
9:30 p.m.

The controllers use binoculars to help them see better, especially when the weather is bad.

The instrument panel tells air traffic controllers how many planes are in the area, whether they're taking off, landing or just flying past, what speeds they're going, and how high up they are.

The small plane flies west, with the huge dark lake to the left, land to the right. Ahead the pilot can see the city, spread out like a carpet of light. Out on the lake he sees red, blue and white lights. This is the Toronto City Centre Airport.

When the aircraft is five miles away, the pilot radios the air traffic controller and stays in contact until he's landed and parked. Radar can't pick up anything flying lower than five hundred feet, so most of the time controllers use their eyesight. In bad weather, pilots use computers to help them "see" the runway. Flying planes and directing air traffic are jobs that carry a lot of responsibility. One mistake could be serious—or at least give someone a cold bath in the lake!

Tonight the weather is clear and traffic is light. The control tower gives the *City of Mississauga* permission to land, and the pilot guides the plane down onto the runway. He's come home.

Commercial pilots are only allowed to work 14 hours per shift. If they get too tired they are more likely to make mistakes.

The Theatre
10:00 p.m.

Anna-Louise Richardson applies her stage makeup before the show.

The stage manager's booth. Kevin Bowers controls the lights and sound from here.

A pair of doors open wide, and excited people flow out into the street, laughing, talking, and interrupting each other. This is The Factory Theatre.

Now the play is over and the actors are in their dressing rooms, changing into street clothes and talking about the show. They're a little sad, because the play's run is finished, and they might never play these characters again.

Stage actors work mostly at night.

In the auditorium, the stagehands are starting "tear-down". They have to clear the stage of props, take apart the set, and take down the lights. Since everything has to be put carefully away, they'll be here for a long time. So will the wardrobe and "property" staff: they have to look after all the objects used in the play. The costumes have to be washed or sent to the cleaners, and all the furniture and other items must be packed and labelled.

At last everything is done, and they can go home, the very last to leave the building. The doors are locked, voices call goodnight, and the theatre is left silent and dark. The play is over.

The Concert
10:30 pm

The sound-mixer sits at a dark console during the concert, making sure that the volume and balance of sound are right.

The concert is coming to an end. Jesse Cook and his band have played for over two hours, but they hate to stop.

Jesse is a night person. He feels that people are more open to music at night, so this is one of his favourite times for composing and performing. He often doesn't get to bed before four o'clock in the morning.

Many people in the music industry are busy at night. If musicians play at night, their technicians and "roadies" have to work too. So do the staff at the clubs or theatres where they are performing. When musicians record at night, the sound engineers at the recording studio have to be there.

Musicians like to sleep in, but sometimes they have to do early-morning interviews! Luckily they are good at sleeping wherever they are—in hotel lobbies, on buses or planes…

The band plays its second encore. Now it really is time to go.

Jesse has performed in all sorts of clubs and theatres during his career.

Union Station
11:00 p.m.

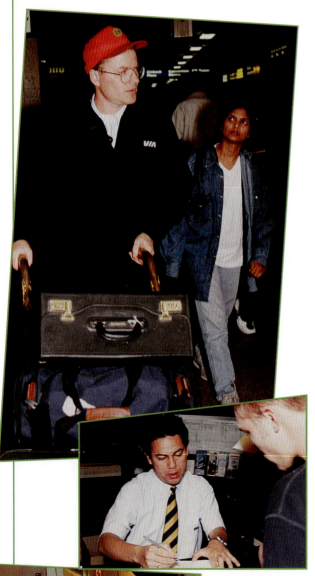

It's late in the evening. Most of the passengers have gone, and the shops and snack bars are closing up for the night. The last train of the day is about to leave.

Most North American cities have one grand railway station built around 1900. They are usually made of stone and have huge halls, high ceilings and lots of decoration. For the first few decades of this century, people going long distances travelled on the trains.

If these marble walls could talk, they could tell us about young people who went west to seek their fortunes and immigrant families looking for homes in an unknown land.

The crew of the last train heads for the boarding area: two engineers, two train crew conductors, two servers for the dining car, and two passenger conductors. The porters, sometimes called Red Caps, help people with their luggage and take them to the train.

Soon the platform guard's whistle will scream, and the train will move off into the night.

Sarah's Café
11:30 p.m.

The late movie is over, and a group of hungry people is strolling through the streets. Someone suggests going to Sarah's for a bite to eat, and everyone cheers.

Sarah's Café is open late. It's a welcoming, cozy place, and neighbourhood people are in the habit of dropping in to talk to each other.

There are a lot of regular customers. Some stay for hours, nibbling on snacks, sipping a coffee and chatting with the staff. They come in so often that they've become friends.

The night workers at the café have plenty to do in addition to talking to customers: they prepare and cook the food, make the coffee, pour the drinks, wait on tables, and work the cash register.

The waitress brings the plates from the kitchen. The steaming food smells wonderful, and everyone sighs as they pick up their forks. It's a great way to finish the evening.

Sheila Nolan, the owner, likes the food to look as good as it tastes.

Hotel Bonaventure
12:00 a.m.

The night operator finds that sleepless guests sometimes just want a little chat.

Most of the guests are asleep, and the lobby is almost empty. People come and go at all hours of the day and night, but this evening the staff of the Montreal Bonaventure are enjoying some quiet time.

This hotel is unusual: it is located on the 17th floor of a convention centre. The doorman—the first person guests will meet—welcomes people downstairs. Then there is a bellman, who helps carry the luggage. Upstairs, the staff at the reception desk check in the new visitors.

Outside on the roof there is a heated swimming pool. People can swim there in the wintertime, with snowflakes drifting down onto their heads. There is also an acre of parkland! It has trees and plants, a pond, and even ducks and pheasants.

A limousine pulls up downstairs. "Bon soir," says the doorman. "Did you have a good flight?" The crew of a European plane has just arrived. They stay here in between flights, since they have to work again the next day.

"Yes, thank you," they say. They are looking forward to a good night's sleep.

The bilingual doorman greeting new arrivals.

The popular lunch bar is deserted at this hour.

The Hospital
12:30 a.m.

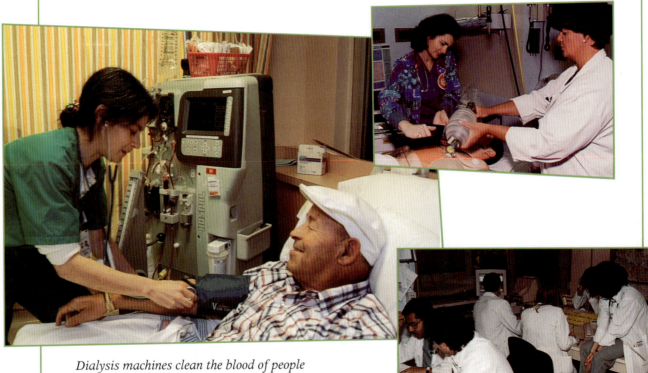

Dialysis machines clean the blood of people whose kidneys don't work.

A siren screams in the night. An ambulance with flashing lights races around the corner and stops in front of the Emergency Department entrance.

A man on a stretcher is carried inside. He collapsed on the sidewalk, and people on the street called an ambulance right away. Now the nurses and doctors are working at top speed to find out what's wrong.

Other parts of the hospital are awake too. The dialysis department, which treats patients with kidney disease, certainly is. In some hospitals there is such a demand for these machines that they run 24 hours a day.

The man in the emergency room opens his eyes, and the staff smile with relief. As they ask him questions and make arrangements to get him a bed, another ambulance brakes at the door. It's just the beginning of a long night.

Times Square
1:00 a.m.

It's late at night, but Times Square is wide awake! This place might be called the heart of New York City. Right in the middle of the theatre district, it's located just a few blocks from Central Park and some of New York's greatest museums and art galleries. Times Square is crossed by one of the most famous streets in the world: Broadway.

Actually, Times Square isn't square at all. It's five blocks long, and every side of it is lined with shops, movie theatres and snack bars. Most of these places stay open all night.

A cop in Times Square sees a lot of life on the night shift. This officer has worked at his job for many years, and he loves it. He's talked to all kinds of people and seen all kinds of things in his time, from break-dancing street kids to organ-grinders' monkeys. The night may be long, but in New York it's never boring!

Horse-drawn carriage rides are a popular pastime with tourists and New Yorkers alike.

Millions of visitors come to New York, and sooner or later most of them end up in Times Square.

Times Square got its name from the old New York Times *newspaper building. It's still there, but now it has a huge electronic sign stretching across the top. The sign shows the latest news headlines.*

A Newspaper
1:30 a.m.

It's halfway through the night shift. Everything is normal: the news was updated an hour ago, the huge printing machines are spinning, and the floor of the press room is covered in a layer of ink.

Stop the presses! An important news story has come in from the other side of the world. Now the front page must be changed to squeeze in the new headline, photograph and story. This will take about ten minutes.

There's a lot of repetition on this job, so the excitement is welcome. Late-breaking news helps keep the folder man, ink men, reel men and paper handlers on the alert.

The newspaper, with brand-new headlines, is beginning to run again. The out-of-town editions go first, and they'll be loaded onto trucks heading for the expressway. The local edition comes next, hitting the street as the sun rises over the city. Now morning is only a few hours away.

Checking a page layout.

The newsroom at night.

Loading paper on the press. Web presses print on one gigantic roll of paper instead of separate sheets.

Checking four-colour film

The Street Patrol
2:00 a.m.

The streets are home to many people in every big North American city.

It's the middle of the night, and a woman is sitting in a doorway with a blanket around her shoulders. A van comes around the corner and stops at the curb.

"Hi, there," the driver says. "Do you want any food?" The woman nods her head. Another worker gives the woman some hot soup and a sandwich, and asks about her cough.

The Anishnawbe Street Patrol in Toronto has more work all the time: a few years ago they served 11,534 homeless people, and now the number is over 42,000. In the winter, the Patrol works every day and every night—all night. The staff give out sleeping bags, blankets, clothes, food, and information about AIDS. They give first aid, see to it that people get medical care when it's needed, and offer access to counselling, shelters and detox centres. Twice a week a nurse comes along to do things like vaccinations and TB tests.

The Street Patrol workers get back in the van and drive on. There will be many more people to see before the night is over.

The nurse gives a flu shot to a young man living on the street.

This man is glad to have a newspaper as well as a comforter.

The Subway
2:30 a.m.

This woman is a power-cut monitor and track maintainer.

The "tie-plates" that line the floor are being replaced to re-insulate the track signal system.

The last train of the night has vanished into the tunnel, sweeping a damp, chilly wind behind it. The platforms are empty and quiet. A few hours from now, this station will fill again with musicians playing for the crowds, kids heading to school—all kinds of people beginning their day. But now, in the middle of the night, the only people here are the workers down *below* the platform.

They are upgrading the track system, starting with the busiest stations. Eventually there will be new tie-plates installed on every bit of the city's 94 kilometres (about 64 miles) of subway track.

Now a special train comes through to collect garbage from each station, and the repairmen climb up off the track. The disposal crew has to work quickly, since there are many more stations to go. The trains will start running again at 5:36, and the first sleepy passengers will stumble in, clutching their cups of coffee.

The night shift is half over.

24-Hour Grocery Store
3:00 a.m.

Pricing fruit.

Working at the deli counter.

The streets of this friendly neighbourhood are still alive, even at this hour. This is an area with an interesting mix of people—students live next door to professors, and there are immigrants, young families, lawyers and streetcar drivers. The Supersave sees them all.

The staff here restock the shelves, keep the colourful displays neatly arranged, clean the counters, and chat with the customers strolling in from the night.

The busiest time is past now. People heading home from an evening out stopped in a few hours ago. Then came the trickle of footsore wait-staff from the restaurants and pubs. Now the cab drivers come in, and sleepless neighbours wander the aisles looking for the junk food. The staff mop the floor and whistle along with the radio. It's a typical night at the Supersave.

Restocking the shelves.

35

The All-Night Bus
3:30 a.m.

Much of the city is asleep. The subways stopped running over an hour ago. But Yonge St., which runs right through Toronto, is busy all night. From the lake at the bottom of the route to Steeles Ave. at the top, people are waiting for the all-night bus.

The driver has worked this route for four years. She knows her regular passengers and where they get off. Sometimes she wakes them up so they don't ride past their stop!

Things can get a little out of hand on the night bus once in awhile, but the driver has two emergency buttons. If she pushes one, help will come right away. Mostly, though, she enjoys her job. Her sense of humour helps with that!

The bus pulls over and a tired-looking woman gets on. "I'm glad it's you again," she says. "I always look forward to your smiling face."

The morning is a little closer.

All-night bus drivers keep their energy up by having snacks and coffee. If there is a quiet moment they sometimes get up and stretch their legs.

Earlier in the night, the passengers were mostly people coming home from work or an evening out. By this time, some of them are people on their way to work.

Amy's Bread
4:00 a.m.

Sunrise is still hours away. The city of Manhattan never really goes to sleep, so the streets glitter with light. The woman coming along 9th Avenue looks at her watch and walks a little faster. Her name is Amy Scherber.

She unlocks a door, calling hello as she slings off her jacket. Voices answer from the back. This is Amy's Bread.

There are many kinds of bread, made from recipes from all over the world.

Like the city, the bakery never sleeps. Making bread takes a long time, so people have to work all night to get it ready by morning. Some of their customers are people who need just a loaf or two, but most of them are other companies, like restaurants, that need fresh bread for *their* customers.

The hot bread crackles as the cool air hits it, and a warm, rich smell spreads through the bakery. The night is inching toward morning, and the first customer of the day walks in, ready to take a vanload of bread to feed hungry New Yorkers.

Amy is decorating each raw loaf with little slashes. The patterns help people tell one kind of bread from another.

A Farmers' Market
4:30 a.m.

It's still dark. Soon the farmers' market will begin, and the vendors are hurrying to set up before the doors open.

Some of the bakers, farmers, and butchers had to get up in the middle of the night and drive a long way to get

FARMERS MARKET OPEN EVERY SAT. AT - 5⁰⁰ AM

here in time. Many of them loaded their trucks the evening before, because that part of the work can take up to an hour and a half. Unloading is faster, but they still have to carry all the produce into the building, put up trestle tables and arrange the displays at their stalls.

This market is very popular. Many people enjoy shopping here more than at one big store. It could be for the freshness, good smells, and prices of the things for sale, but they also like buying food from the person who produced it. The market has a special atmosphere, almost like a festival—everyone seems to be having a good time.

The clock strikes five, and the first customers walk in with their baskets and knapsacks. Another Saturday at the market has begun.

Before dawn: set-up time.

Some of the foods sold here are made from family recipes that go back generations.

Metro Morning Radio
5:00 a.m.

A cold wind is blowing off the lake, and the sky shows no hint of morning. The broadcasters hurry along the sidewalk and into the huge headquarters of the CBC. They work on *Metro Morning*, one of the Canadian Broadcasting Corporation's most popular radio shows.

First they warm up with a cup of coffee while they read newspapers and magazines and check out the latest bulletins. It's part of their job to be totally up-to-date on what's going on in the news. Then they review what's ahead for today's show.

Andy Barrie, the host of *Metro Morning*, does as many as nine interviews in one three-hour show. He talks to all kinds of people about what's happening around the city and around the world.

It's getting late—almost time to be moving into the studio, sorting notes and putting the headphones on. The show is about to begin.

Andy Barrie takes a breather as Anubha Parray reads the news.

Bruce Dowbiggin gives the sports scores while Jim Curran waits to do the traffic update.

42

One of the Metro Morning *producers during the broadcast.*

A Construction Site
5:30 a.m.

A passerby peeks at the huge hole dug for a foundation, 40 feet below.

Workers use special caution when moving heavy equipment.

Night is almost over. The sky is slowly getting lighter in the east, and there is a construction worker already on-site.

He is the electrician foreman, and has a lot of work to get through today. He decided to come in early and check that everything is ready for his crew to start without any delays.

On a huge project like this, the construction team can be big. It has a superintendent, a senior project manager, a project co-ordinator, crane operators, hook-up men, forming crews, electricians, plumbers, and many more. The safety man is one of the most important people on the crew. He sees to it that all workers follow the safety rules and wear hardhats and steel-toed boots at all times.

Later in the project will come the crews that finish the interior of the building, like drywallers, finish carpenters and painters. Altogether, it takes up to a year and a half to complete a building this size.

The electrician is satisfied—all his supplies have been delivered, and everything is where it should be. He takes a sip of coffee and greets the workers who have begun to arrive. Morning is coming.

An electrician on the top floor checks the storage of materials.

The Wildlife Centre
6:00 a.m.

Migrating birds smash against lighted sky-scrapers at night, and thousands die every season. Here, FLAP volunteers look for any that are still alive.

Some centres are lucky enough to have veterinarians who volunteer to treat the sickest animals.

It's very early. The first volunteer worker is arriving at the centre. During the busiest times some wildlife rehabilitation centres are open 24 hours a day, but right now there aren't too many animals to look after.

The first thing this volunteer does is check the sick or injured animals, to make sure that they didn't get worse overnight. Next she feeds them and the lost or orphaned animals. After that, she gives medicine to some and changes old bandages. This can be dangerous, because the animals are frightened and sometimes in pain. She'll have to be careful, and will need help handling the bigger animals.

This morning will be very special, because a recovered fox is going to be released. This is the best part of working at the centre!

The staff return the fox to where it was found so it will have the best chance for survival. Volunteers open the cage and step away, watching as the fox gets used to being free again. It sniffs the air and looks around for a moment or two. Then it runs away across the ravine.

The night is over, and the day has begun.

46

Some of the animals can't eat on their own. This hummingbird, for example, has to be fed with an eyedropper.

Acknowledgements

The editors wish to thank the following for their assistance during the preparation of this book:

Amy's Bread, New York—Amy Scherber

Anishnawbe Health Toronto Street Patrol Program—Harvey Manning, Jane Harrison and the staff of the Street Patrol

Aquabus, Vancouver—Jeff Pratt, Paul Barrett and John Vasquez

Bloor Supersave, Toronto—Eric Smith, Mike Poissant and the night staff

Canadian Broadcasting Corporation—Gord Cochrane, Jim Curran, Barb Dickie, Bruce Dowbiggin, Ted Fairhurst, Anubha Parray and Michael Lamb, with special thanks to Andy Barrie

Jesse Cook, Kathleen Shea, Pacy Shulman, Bill Katsioutas, Blake Manning, Arturo Avalos and Etric Lyons

Katharine Creery, consultant

Diffusion Dimedia, Montreal

Factory Theatre, Toronto—David Baile, Tom Bartlett, Kevin Bowers, Ken Gass, Mikki Landau, Karen O'Brien, Dennis O'Connor and Karen Robinson

FLAP (Fatal Light Awareness Program), Toronto—Carolynn Parke

Hotel Bonaventure, Montreal—Margot McFarlane and the night staff

The Kortright Centre, Ontario—Csilla Darvasi and the staff of Wildcare Rehabilitation Centre

Ledcor Industries, Vancouver—Kerry Gillis

Masters Swim Club, Toronto—Heather Davies, Peter Mumford and the East York Masters' Swim Club

Organic Farmers' Market vendors, Toronto

Sarah's Café, Toronto—Sheila Nolan, Pedro Orrego and the night staff

Toronto City Centre Airport—Brent McKellar of Air Ontario, airport staff and Dave Washington of Navigation Canada, with special thanks to Frank Di Carlo, also of Navigation Canada

Toronto Hospital—Josie Pennetta, and special thanks to Marsha Furuya

The Toronto Sun—Bob Sweet, Bob Pulfer, and other members of the *Sun* press room

Toronto Transit Commission—Robert Newman, Brian Drew, Ted Harris, Stephanie Chapman and the TTC staff

Union Station, Toronto—Jim Cook, Diane Graham, Russell Wells and the staff of Union Station